First published by Parragon Books Ltd in 2015

Parragon Books Ltd
Chartist House
15–17 Trim Street
Bath BA1 1HA, UK
www.parragon.com

ISBN 978-1-4748-0836-1

Printed in China

From the movie

Disney

FROZEN

Sisters and Snowmen

PaRragon

Bath · New York · Cologne · Melbourne · Delhi
Hong Kong · Shenzhen · Singapore · Amsterdam

From the movie
Disney
FROZEN

A FROZEN ADVENTURE

The kingdom of Arendelle was a happy place,
located next to a deep fjord. At night, the Northern
Lights often lit up the skies in beautiful patterns.
But the king and queen lived with a secret worry.

Their eldest daughter, Elsa, had magical powers. She could freeze things and create snow, even in the summer!

Their youngest daughter, Anna, just adored her older sister. The two loved to play together in the snowy playgrounds that Elsa created.

One night, Elsa's magic accidentally hit Anna.

The king and queen rushed the girls to the realm of the trolls for some magical help. The trolls advised that Anna would recover. They also advised that Elsa's powers would get stronger, so she should learn to control them.

Back in Arendelle, Elsa struggled to stay in control of her powers at all times. She decided to stay away from Anna, to keep her little sister safe.

The trolls had changed Anna's memories, so she didn't remember Elsa's magic. Instead she grew up thinking that Elsa wanted nothing to do with her.

By the time Elsa was crowned queen, the sisters had grown far apart. They hardly knew each other at all.

Having grown up mostly by herself, Anna had felt lonely for a long time. So she was thrilled to meet handsome Prince Hans on the day of Elsa's coronation.

Anna and Hans liked each other straight away. At the coronation party they danced and talked all night long.

Anna thought it was a great idea to get engaged quickly. But Elsa reacted angrily. "You can't marry someone you've just met!"

Anna argued back. "I can't live like this any more! I'm always alone!"

Then Elsa got upset and an icy blast shot from her hand – in front of everyone!

Worried that her secret was exposed and afraid she would hurt someone, Elsa fled from the castle. Everything froze behind her as she ran away.

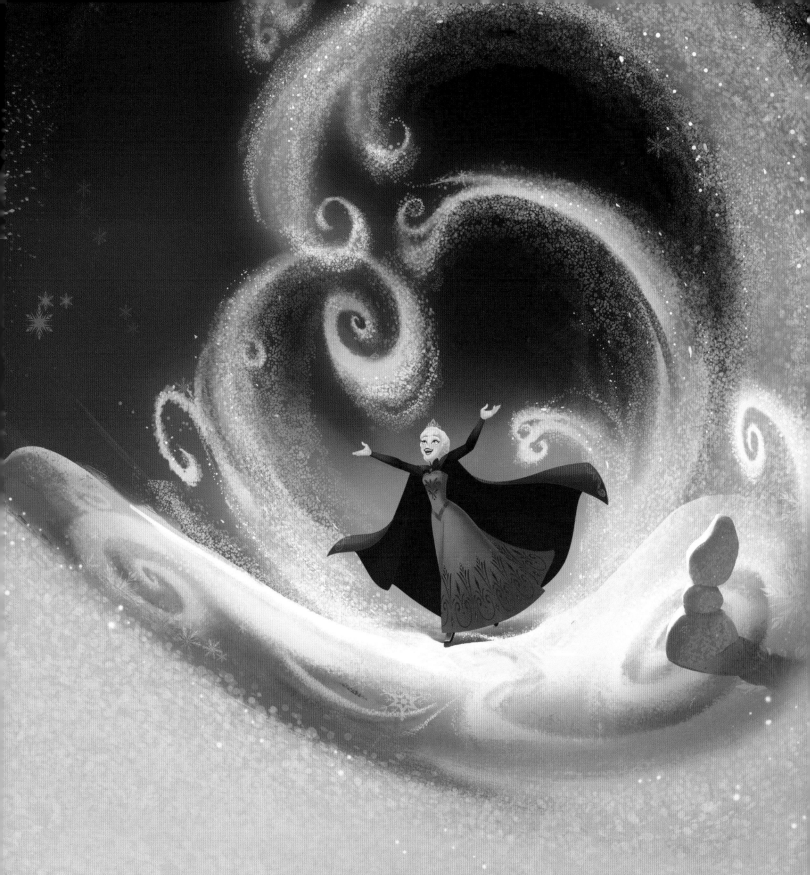

Once Elsa had climbed up into the mountains, she felt calm. Now that she was all alone, she was able to let out her powers for the first time ever! She created whirls of snow, ice and even an ice palace.

She was able to be herself and it felt wonderful!

Meanwhile, Anna realized that Elsa had been acting distant for all those years because she needed to hide her magic. Anna decided to go after Elsa – now that her secret was out, they could be together!

Anna headed up the mountain, but her horse threw her into the snow. Luckily, she was able to find shelter in a nearby shop.

Inside, Anna met a young man covered in frost. He was cross because he was an ice harvester and the mid-summer snowstorm was ruining his business.

He also knew where the storm was coming from. That meant he could take her to Elsa!

Anna hired the young man, who was called Kristoff,
to take her up the North Mountain to find Elsa.
His reindeer, Sven, came along on the journey, too.

As they neared the top of the mountain, the trio saw
a beautiful wintery landscape. Elsa had covered everything
with glistening, sparkling ice.

Elsa had also created
a snowman ... who was alive!

The snowman's name was Olaf and he
was excited to hear that Anna planned
to bring back summer, because he loved
the idea of warm weather.
He offered to take them to Elsa.

As the group moved on they found the fantastic ice palace that Elsa had created with her magical powers.

Anna was impressed by Elsa's powers and sparkling ice palace. But she really wanted Elsa to come back home.

Elsa thought the people of Arendelle wouldn't accept her – and she was still afraid that she would hurt them.

The two girls argued. Although Elsa didn't intend to hurt Anna, she hit her sister in the chest with a blast of ice.

Then she created another snowman, named Marshmallow, who was much bigger than Olaf. The huge snowman made sure that Anna, Kristoff, Sven and Olaf left the mountain quickly!

Once they were safe Kristoff noticed that Anna's hair was turning white. Kristoff took her to the trolls to see if their magic could help.

The trolls explained that Elsa's blast had hit Anna in the heart – and that soon she would freeze completely! But, they added, "An act of true love will thaw a frozen heart."

Olaf and Kristoff decided to hurry Anna back to Arendelle so she could get a true love's kiss from Hans.

Meanwhile, back in Arendelle, Hans helped everyone during the storm. Then Anna's horse arrived back in Arendelle – without her!

Hans took a group out to find Anna ... but they found Elsa first. Elsa was forced to defend herself against some of the men.

Finally, she was taken back to Arendelle as a prisoner! The men were convinced she was dangerous.

Kristoff brought Anna to Arendelle, but Hans refused to kiss her. He didn't love her! He only wanted to rule Arendelle but had to make sure the sisters were out of the way first.

Anna was devastated. But Olaf realized that Kristoff loved Anna – so his kiss could still save her. Anna made her way towards Kristoff. Then she saw her sister in danger....

She threw herself in front of Elsa, just in time to block
a blow from Hans's sword.

At that moment, Anna transformed into solid ice.
The sword shattered against her icy body.

Stunned, Elsa threw her arms round Anna and cried.
She didn't want to lose her sister.

Suddenly, Anna began to melt. Anna's act of true love
for her sister meant that the spell was broken!

Then, with Anna's love and faith, Elsa managed to bring
back summer.

The sisters hugged and promised to love each other from then on. The people of Arendelle saw everything and they welcomed Elsa home.

Kristoff decided to stay in Arendelle and so did Olaf – with the help of a little winter cloud to keep him cool. Best of all, the sisters were back together and happy at last!

From the movie
Disney
FROZEN

A Sister More Like Me

Written by Barbara Jean Hicks

Illustrated by Brittney Lee

My name is
Princess Elsa.
I'm as royal as can be.

If the words look neat
and simple, then they
belong to me.

I'm her little sister,
Anna – I like colour,
noise and sunshine.

When the words are bold
and crowded, you can tell
that they are mine.

When you and I were little,
we were close as we could be.

I was happy you were Anna.
You were thrilled that I was me.

Till I had to hide my magic,
and our closeness
had to end.

I was still your older sister,
but I couldn't be your friend.

I followed you
around the house

and chattered like a bird.

I tried my best to please you,
but you never said a word.

That's when I started dreaming
about how my life would be ...
if I ever had a chance to have
a sister more like me.

I considered it my job to do
what needed to be done.
You were always and forever
finding ways to have more fun.

There were times you made me crazy,
though I tried to let you be,
as I wondered why I couldn't have
a sister more like me.

While I galloped on my pony
in the wind and rain and sun,
you were cooped up in the library –
and you thought that it was fun!

I'd have loved to have a playmate
who would join me up a tree.
I would have, if I could have had
a sister more like me.

And *I'd* have loved to have a friend who knew how to study,
I would have, if I could have had a sister more like *me*.

You needed peace
and quiet.

I was Princess Meet-and-Greet.

Your room was an explosion!

Mine was always clean and neat.

You were elegant and proper,
and you loved a fancy tea,

while I preferred a bright and
breezy picnic by the sea.

You didn't seem to care a bit about the way you dressed.
It was important, as a princess, that I looked my best.

You were the picture of perfection,
every day, no matter what.
I tried to understand you,
but the door was always shut.

Then one day I was
so dazzled when I saw
what you could be.
And I wondered ...
did I *really* want a
sister more like me?

You showed me that you loved me,
and I suddenly felt free —
and truly glad I didn't have
a sister more like me.

You always did your duty,
and you always used your head.

You always listened to your heart
and followed where it led.

I'm very glad I *haven't* had a sister more like me.

With you around, without a doubt, I see things differently.

I was prickly as an urchin.

I was stubborn as a mule!
Now we try to work together –

it's our Sister Golden Rule.

You are bold and fearless, Sister,
and you have a loving heart.

You are poised and graceful, Sister,
and so wonderfully smart.

I'm so happy you are Anna and I'm pleased that I am me.

I'm thrilled that you are Elsa and I'm happy I am me!

But even more important — we are happy we are WE.

From the movie
Disney
FROZEN

An Amazing Snowman

Written by Barbara Jean Hicks

illustrated by Olga T. Mosqueda

Olaf is not
your everyday
snowman.

He
walks.

He
talks.

He even sings.

But those aren't the only things that make him special!

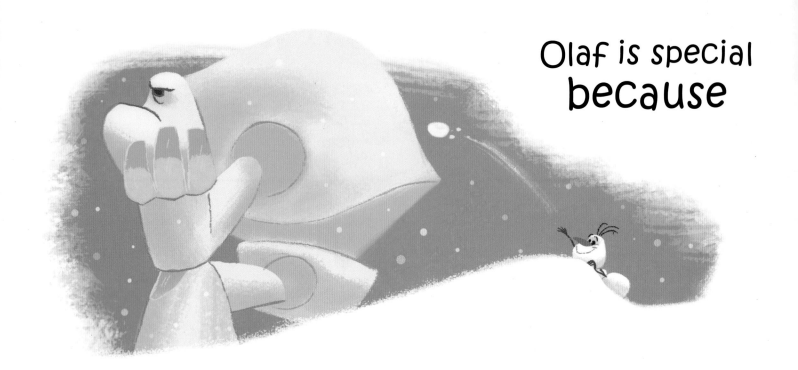

Olaf is special **because**

he sees the **best in everyone.**

His brother, Marshmallow, is a playful fellow....

Sven the reindeer
is forever trying to
kiss his nose ...

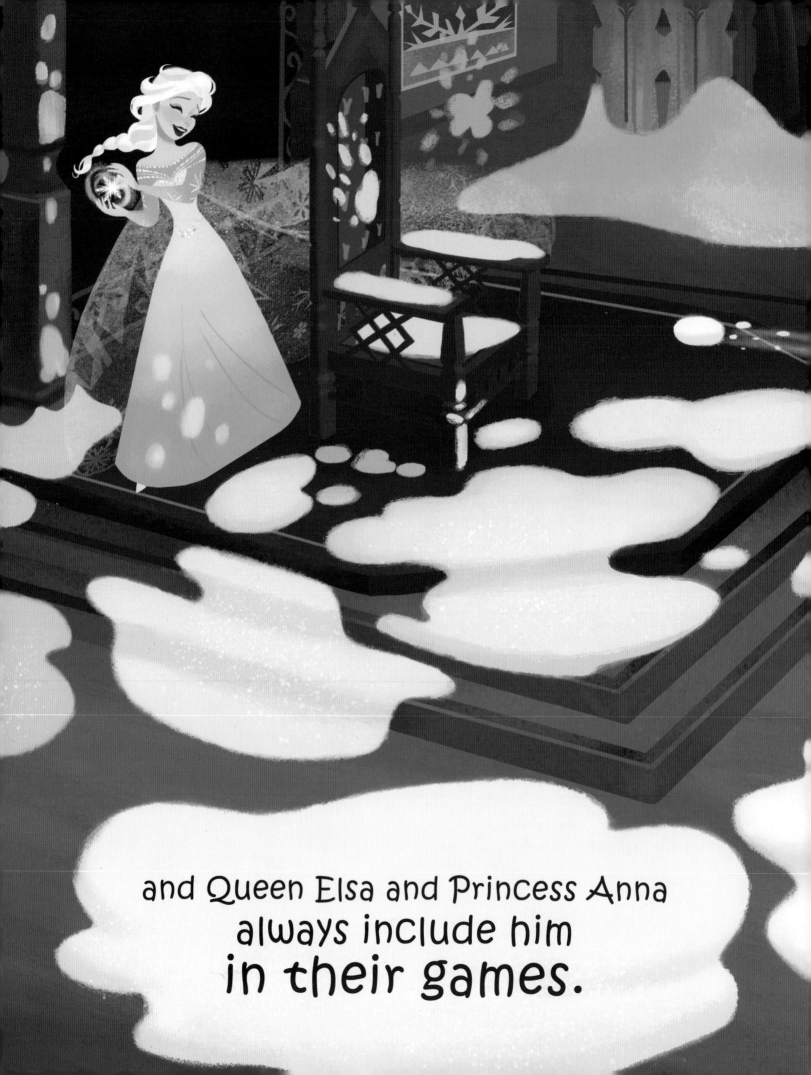

and Queen Elsa and Princess Anna
always include him
in their games.

Olaf is special
because

he finds
beauty in
every day ...

and because he dreams.

and ships sailing to new horizons ...

Olaf dreams about soaring in the sky …

and picking fresh fruit ...

Olaf is
special
because
in his
eyes,
summer

or winter,

every day is an adventure ...

and
every
night
shines.

Olaf is
special because
he knows
that every
ending ...

... is a chance for a new beginning ...

and a chance ...
for a
nice warm
hug!

The
End